It was cold in the Stone Age.
When the icy wind blew it was freezing.

"I really do need something to keep my bottom warm," Pod told his Dad.

"You could make something," Dad said.

"Stone is very handy."

Pod **smashed** and **chiselled**.

He **chipped** and **sanded**.

Pod made himself some super stone underpants.

"Yahoo! These are great!"
He put them on and went out
to play.

His friends were cross.
"Oh Pod! Now they've scored a goal!"

"Yahoo! GOAL!"

the other team shouted.

Pod and his friends went to the lake. They all jumped in. His friends **bobbed** back up.

But Pod sank down.

...SPLINTERY!

"Ow!"

In the night Pod's wooden underpants mysteriously disappeared.

"Stone's no good. Wood's no use. But I still need some bottom warmers!"
What could he use now?

Shells were too **clattery**.

Spider webs were too **sticky**.

Mud was too **yucky**.

Pod searched for feathers.
Not every bird wanted to share.

At last Pod had enough feathers.

He **wove** and he **cut**. He **plaited** and he **sewed**.

The fluffy
feather underpants
were light and soft and
deliciously warm.

When he played football he could...**run**

...**jump**

...**and kick.**

But...

He **twitched** and **twisted**.
He **squirmed** and **wriggled**.
The feathers tickled him so much he missed
the ball and bounced headfirst into a swamp.

The feather underpants
were too **ticklish** for Pod...

But his mum really liked them.

What a lovely feather duster!

Pod's bottom was
still cold, but...

Hoosh Hoosh

"Hello warm, woolly mammoth," said Pod.
"Ooo! Your coat's given me a great idea!"

Pod's needles **clicked** and **clacked**.
He **knitted** and **knotted**.

Pod loved his new **woolly underpants**.

Now climbing trees was a **doddle**.

Kicking balls was **brilliant**.

Swimming was **super**.

And best of all...

"My bottom is so
TOASTY!"

The End

Maverick
arts publishing
www.maverickbooks.co.uk

Stone Underpants
an original concept by
'16 Rebecca Lisle

Rebecca Lisle
chard Watson

ecord for this book is available at the

Published by MAVERICK ARTS PUBLISHING LTD

Studio 3A, City Business Centre, 6 Brighton Road,
Horsham, West Sussex, RH13 5BB
© Maverick Arts Publishing Limited November 2016
+44 (0)1403 256941

ISBN 978-1-84886-221-0